JONATHAN EMMETT

WANDA WALLABY FINDS HER BOUNCE

ILLUSTRATED BY
MARK CHAMBERS

BLOOMSBURY

LONDON BERLIN NEW YORK SYDNEY

Wanda Wallaby was a wonderful WALKER but . . .

she could not **HOP** like
the other wallabies.

Whenever she tried, she just fell over.

'You can do it,' her father told her. 'You just need to find your BOUNCE!'

'What does my "bounce" LOOK like?' asked Wanda, searching around for it.

'I can't tell you that,' said her father, laughing,
'but you'll know when you've found it.
Just you wait and see!'

But Wanda could not wait. And she was sure that if her bounce was anywhere near, she would have found it by now.

So, early the next morning, while her father was sleeping, she set off into the trees to look for it.

Wanda searched high and low among the trees.
But she didn't find her bounce. She DID find
a spiny anteater snuffling around the roots.

'Can you help me?' asked
Wanda. 'I'm trying to
find my bounce.'

'What does it SMELL like?' asked the
anteater, wrinkling his long nose.

'I can't tell you,' said Wanda.

'Then I can't help you,' said the anteater. 'Have you
looked in the cave?'

Wanda searched the cave from front to back.
But she didn't find her bounce. She DID find
a bat hanging from the ceiling.

'Can you help me?' asked Wanda.
'I'm trying to find my bounce.'

'What does it SOUND like?' asked the bat, twitching her large ears.

'I can't tell you,' said Wanda.

'Then I can't help you,' said the bat. 'Have you looked in the clearing?'

Wanda searched all around the clearing. But she didn't find her bounce. She DID find a mole burrowing out of the ground.

'Can you help me?' asked Wanda. 'I'm trying to find my bounce.'

'What does it FEEL like?' asked the mole, flexing his big paws.

'I can't tell you,' said Wanda.

'Then I can't help you,' said the mole. 'Have you looked in the creek?'

Wanda searched up and down the creek. But she didn't find her bounce. She **DID** find a crafty crocodile lazing in the water.

'Can you help me?' asked Wanda. 'I'm trying to find my bounce.'

'What does it TASTE like?' asked the crafty crocodile, licking his long lips.

'I can't tell you,' sighed Wanda, who was ready to give up and go home.

'Well, I CAN tell you,' said the crafty crocodile, 'because I've just eaten it!'

'You've EATEN my bounce?' gasped Wanda.

'Well not quite EATEN,' said the crafty crocodile.

'It got stuck at the back of my mouth. It's very uncomfortable. You'd be doing me a favour if you took it out.'

Wanda peered through the crocodile's long pointed teeth into the darkness at the back of his mouth.

'I can't see anything,' she said.

'You won't see it from there. You'll have to get in,' said the crafty crocodile, opening his jaws wide.

And Wanda – who wanted her bounce SO badly – climbed inside.

SNAP! went the crocodile's mouth. But at that moment, Wanda realised she had been tricked and without thinking what she was doing

she
HOPPED
back out.

'There was NOTHING in there!' said Wanda accusingly.

'Nothing but a foolish young wallaby,' snarled the crocodile, lurching after her.

But he was too late.
Wanda was already
HOPPING away.

Wanda Wallaby was a wonderful walker . . .

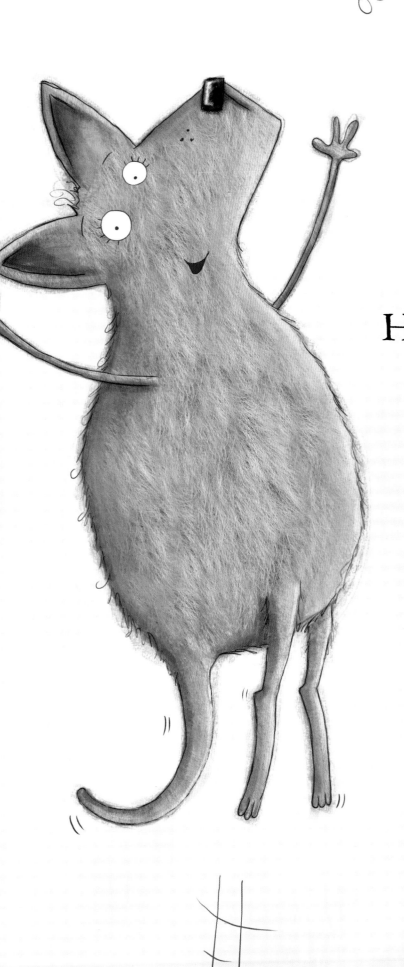

and now
she was a
high-jumping
HOPPER as well.

'I suppose there was SOMETHING in that crocodile's mouth,' thought Wanda, as she hopped home happily.

'After all, it was where
I found my BOUNCE!'

FUN ANIMAL Facts

All the animals in this story live in Australia. Here are a few fun facts about each of them.

A wallaby looks like a small kangaroo. After it is born, a baby wallaby spends several months living in a pouch on its mother's tummy. Young wallabies, like Wanda, are known as 'joeys' – just like their young kangaroo cousins.

Wallaby

Spiny anteaters are also known as 'echidnas'. As well as long noses, they have long, sticky tongues which are perfect for catching the ants and other insects they eat. If scared, they can roll up into a tight, prickly ball.

Spiny anteater

Inland cave bats can be found living in caves and on rocky outcrops all over Australia. They can't see very well but are able to find their way around by calling out and then listening to the echoes with their large ears.

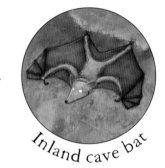

Inland cave bat

The marsupial mole is almost completely blind but feels its way around using large shovel-like paws. Like many Australian animals, it has a pouch to carry its babies. But the marsupial mole's pouch faces backwards so that it doesn't fill up with earth as it digs its tunnels.

Marsupial mole

Although smaller than other Australian crocodiles, the freshwater crocodile can move faster on land than any other crocodile, running at speeds of up to 17 km per hour. Luckily they are not man-eaters, but they do eat wallabies like Wanda!

Freshwater crocodile